Symbols, Landmarks, and Monuments

The Empire State Building

Tamara L. Britton
ABDO Publishing Company

visit us at
www.abdopub.com

Published by ABDO Publishing Company, 4940 Viking Drive, Edina, Minnesota 55435. Copyright © 2005 by Abdo Consulting Group, Inc. International copyrights reserved in all countries. No part of this book may be reproduced in any form without written permission from the publisher. The Checkerboard Library™ is a trademark and logo of ABDO Publishing Company.

Printed in the United States.

Cover Photo: Corbis
Interior Photos: Corbis pp. 1, 5, 6-7, 9, 12, 13, 15, 17, 18, 19, 20, 21, 22, 25, 26, 27, 29; Getty Images p. 23; Library of Congress pp. 8, 10, 11

Series Coordinator: Heidi M. Dahmes
Editors: Heidi M. Dahmes, Megan Murphy
Art Direction & Maps: Neil Klinepier

Special thanks to The Skyscraper Museum, 39 Battery Place, New York, NY 10280, www.skyscraper.org, for the image that appears on page 28.

Library of Congress Cataloging-in-Publication Data

Britton, Tamara L., 1963-
  The Empire State Building / Tamara L. Britton.
    p. cm. -- (Symbols, landmarks, and monuments)
  Includes index.
  ISBN 1-59197-834-3
  1. Empire State Building (New York, N.Y.)--Juvenile literature. 2. New York (N.Y.)--Buildings, structures, etc.--Juvenile literature. I. Title.

F128.8.E46B75 2005
974.7'1--dc22

2004054873

Contents

Famous Landmark 4
Fast Facts 6
Timeline 7
The People 8
The Place 12
The Plan 14
The Construction 16
Tallest Building 22
Money Problems 24
Symbol of America 26
Standing Tall 28
Glossary 30
Web Sites 31
Index 32

The Empire State Building

Famous Landmark

The Empire State Building is one of New York City's most famous landmarks. People arriving by land, sea, or air can always pick out its distinctive shape. It stands out among the towering buildings of the city's skyline.

The building was constructed during the **Great Depression**. The project employed thousands of people during a time when jobs were scarce. When finished, the building boasted 102 floors and was 1,250 feet (381 m) tall!

Since its opening, millions of people have visited the observation deck on the 86th floor. The building has had its share of celebrity visitors, too. Even British royalty and the president of Indonesia have seen the view from the top!

For almost 40 years, the Empire State Building was the tallest building in the world. It became one of the city's most recognizable landmarks. It is a symbol of New York City and the **ingenuity** and determination of those who built it.

The Empire State Building has dominated the New York skyline for almost 75 years.

Fast Facts

√ Sir Edmund Hillary, who climbed Mount Everest in 1953, called the Empire State Building New York's "man-made Everest."

√ The 86th floor was often used to broadcast radio specials. In 1956, a radio show linked the Empire State Building with the world's greatest television and radio towers. The towers were the Eiffel Tower in Paris, a radio tower in Berlin, and a television tower in Stuttgart, Germany.

√ During the construction of the Empire State Building, a nurse and a doctor were on full-time duty at the site. The contractor also built cafeterias on several floors so workers could eat in the building.

√ The Empire State Building has developed an annual lighting schedule that honors national holidays, seasons, and the many ethnic groups living in the New York City area. At night, the building is lit from the 72nd floor up to the base of the antenna.

Timeline

1928	√	The Waldorf-Astoria Hotel was sold to Bethlehem Engineering Corporation; John Jakob Raskob and Alfred E. Smith bought the site when that deal fell through.
1929	√	On August 29, Smith announced his plan to build the tallest building in the world.
1930	√	Construction on the Empire State Building began.
1931	√	The building opened May 1.
1939	√	World War II began.
1941	√	The United States joined the war.
1951	√	The building was sold for $34 million.
1972	√	The Empire State Building lost its title as the tallest building in the world to the World Trade Center.
1986	√	The Empire State Building was recognized as a national historic landmark.

The Empire State Building

The People

Alfred E. Smith was born in New York City in 1873. His family was poor. When his father died, Smith left school and got a job to help support his family.

The New York neighborhood where Alfred E. Smith grew up

Smith worked hard. In 1903, he was elected New York state representative. In 1918, he was elected governor. Even as governor, Smith remembered what it was like to be a poor worker. He fought for better working conditions in factories, better housing, child welfare, and city parks.

John Jakob Raskob was born in 1879 in Lockport, New York. By age 21, he was named assistant to the treasurer of a famous chemical manufacturing company. Raskob advanced quickly there. He was soon in charge of the company's finances.

Alfred E. Smith

Pierre S. du Pont and John Jakob Raskob

In 1913, Raskob and his boss, Pierre S. du Pont, bought **stock** in General Motors Corporation. Raskob became president and finance committee chairman two years later. Under his direction, General Motors dramatically increased its sales and earnings.

Like Smith, Raskob also believed in helping the working class. So, he created the General Motors Acceptance Corporation. This branch of General Motors allowed people to buy cars on **credit**. His **foresight** made him a rich man.

The General Motors Building in Detroit, Michigan

Raskob and Smith became friends through their mutual interest in the Democratic Party. Raskob eventually resigned from General Motors to serve as chairman of the Democratic National Committee.

In 1928, Smith was nominated as the Democratic Party's candidate for president. Raskob managed Smith's campaign. However, Herbert Hoover won the election. So, both Raskob and Smith needed jobs. What they would do next was a big surprise.

The Place

The Waldorf-Astoria Hotel had opened in 1897 at Fifth Avenue and Thirty-Fourth Street in New York City. It was owned by the wealthy Astor family. The hotel was an elegant, expensive place for rich and famous people to stay.

But as time passed, styles changed and the Waldorf-Astoria's popularity declined. In 1928, it was sold to Bethlehem Engineering Corporation. This group of investors wanted to construct an office building on the site. They would call it the Waldorf-Astoria Office Building.

Shreve, Lamb & Harmon was the firm hired to design the building. Unfortunately, Bethlehem Engineering was unable to make payments on the property. The deal fell through. So, Raskob and another group of investors bought the site.

The Waldorf-Astoria Hotel in 1903

The group formed a corporation to finance their building. It was called Empire State Inc. Smith was named president. On August 29, 1929, he publicly announced his plan for the Empire State Building. He said it would be the tallest building in the world.

In the late 1920s, many people were racing to build the world's tallest building. Walter P. Chrysler's Chrysler Building (right) was 77 stories and 1,048 feet (319 m) tall. The Bank of Manhattan Building was 71 stories and 925 feet (282 m) tall.

The Empire State Building

The Plan

The Waldorf-Astoria Hotel had an excellent location at a busy intersection on Fifth Avenue. The site was served by public transportation. It was also near shops, museums, and entertainment. Raskob believed this made it a good spot for an office building.

Empire State Inc. kept Shreve, Lamb & Harmon as **architects** for their building. But, they changed the design created for the Waldorf-Astoria Office Building. They wanted their building to be **unique**. The Empire State Building would be 85 **stories** and 1,050 feet (320 m) tall.

Raskob and Smith wanted the building to be sleek, modern, and well lit. It was designed to look even taller than it was. The top 14 floors would be aluminum, glass, and steel. This would add to the building's clean, stately look.

Smith chose Starrett Brothers & Eken to build the structure. The firm had built the New York Life and Bank of Manhattan buildings. Smith knew the company could work fast and do a good job.

Fifth Avenue in the 1920s was an exciting place. Empire State Inc. knew they had made an excellent decision when they chose this location for the "tallest building in the world."

The Empire State Building

The Construction

The designers and builders of the Empire State Building faced a challenge. They needed to make its interior into good rental space. The high-class tenants Empire State Inc. hoped to attract would not rent a dark, closed-up space. So, the building's interior needed to be light and open.

This was hard to do in skyscrapers. Typically, high-rises were built so the walls carried most of the weight of the building. This meant the walls needed to be thick. But, this also made the windows small and few.

The designers decided to shift the weight to steel columns along the outside of the building. Then, the walls could be thinner and the windows bigger. This would allow more natural light onto each floor.

All the space near the windows needed to be prime rental space. So the elevators, plumbing, and utility systems would be built into a central core. The design also called for elevators that used the bank system.

Empire State Building Statistics

Cornerstone: Original laid by Alfred E. Smith on September 17, 1930

Excavation: Began January 22, 1930

Construction: Began March 17, 1930

Masonry: Began June 1930 and was completed in November of the same year

Total time to build: 1 year and 45 days, including Sundays and holidays

Hours to build: 7,000,000

Workers: Approximately 5,000

Cost: $40,948,900, which included the land

Area of the site: 79,288 square feet (7,366 sq m), or about 2 acres (1 ha)

Total height: 1,454 feet (443 m) to the top of the lightning rod

Floors: 103

Steps: 1,860 from street level to the 102nd floor

Weight: 365,000 tons (331,122 t)

Exterior materials: 200,000 cubic feet (5,663 cubic m) of Indiana limestone, 10,000 square feet (929 sq m) of marble, 60,000 tons (54,431 t) of steel and 10 million bricks

Windows: 6,500

Entrances: 5

Elevators: 73. It is possible to ride from the lobby to the 80th floor in 45 seconds.

This system would use several elevators on the first floor. But, the number of elevators would decrease on the upper floors. In order to use fewer elevators, city codes had to be amended. The top elevator speed was changed from 700 feet per minute (213 m/min) to 1,200 feet per minute (366 m/min).

Before the Empire State Building could be built, the Waldorf-Astoria Hotel had to be **demolished**. Six hundred men worked around the clock to tear down the building. They carted 28,529 truckloads of earth, rock, steel, and debris from the site. By January 1930, the grand old hotel was gone.

Next, construction crews prepared the site for the new building. Builders blasted into rock with dynamite and dug holes to pour the concrete footings. The footings held the 210 steel columns that supported the building. Twelve went all the way to the top!

Alfred E. Smith lays the cornerstone of the Empire State Building on September 17, 1930.

Smith wanted to build a mooring mast for airships at the top of the Empire State Building. This would increase the building's profits, and make it 1,250 feet (381 m) tall. But, heavy winds made the mooring mast extremely risky, so no airships ever docked there. The mast was eventually converted into a television antenna, which made the building 1,472 feet (449 m) tall.

Starrett Brothers & Eken created a tight schedule. Building materials were only delivered when needed. They included steel from Pennsylvania, limestone from Indiana, and wood from the Pacific Northwest.

For each floor, numbered **girders** were **riveted** into place. This steel skeleton was fireproofed with paint, concrete, and brickwork. Next, it was covered with an aluminum frame. The limestone was fit into the aluminum frame, and then the windows were installed.

The job was often perilous, and the pace was quickened to meet the spring deadline. But, Starrett Brothers made sure its workers were treated well. They insisted on taking all safety precautions. There were only five deaths reported during the building's construction.

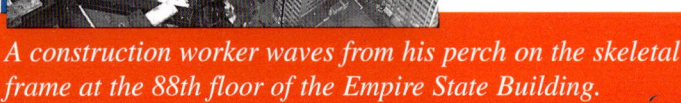
A construction worker waves from his perch on the skeletal frame at the 88th floor of the Empire State Building.

The Empire State Building rose at an amazing four and a half floors a week. The building was completed in record time and under budget. The Empire State Building opened on May 1, 1931.

Most of the materials for the Empire State Building were from the United States. However, the marble came all the way from Europe.

The Empire State Building

Tallest Building

The first year, 775,000 visitors came to see the Empire State Building. The 86th-floor observation deck was popular with tourists and New Yorkers alike. From there, people could see for miles around. It was the best view in town.

Tenants of the Empire State Building had the best address in town. They could take care of most business right in the building. There were restaurants, a dentist, a bank, and a barbershop. There was even a nurse on duty to treat both workers and visitors.

Acrobats perform on the ledge of the Empire State Building in 1934.

Tenants included law offices, insurance companies, and clothing manufacturers. Smith and Raskob had offices there. But, offices in the building were not rented as quickly as they had hoped.

Visitors to the Empire State Building observation deck have a great view at 1,050 feet (320 m) up. By the end of 1976, the Empire State Building had welcomed 50 million visitors.

The Empire State Building

Money Problems

The **Great Depression** finally caught up to the real estate market. Raskob had trouble renting space in the building. Fifty-six of its eighty-six rentable floors did not have tenants. In fact, the building was 75 percent empty in 1933.

Despite the extensive wealth of many of its investors, the Empire State Building was in financial trouble. With no **revenue** coming in, Raskob and Smith had difficulty paying the building's bills. A year and a half after the building opened, they still had made no profit.

Smith asked the city to reduce the building's tax bill. But it was not enough. Empire State Inc. **defaulted** on the **mortgage** loan. Smith asked Metropolitan Life, the mortgage lender, to restructure the loan. Empire State Inc. was heading toward bankruptcy.

In 1939, **World War II** began. Two years later, the United States entered the war. War spending helped the

economy. After the war, the real estate market improved. By 1950, the Empire State Building was fully occupied. It was earning $10 million a year in profit. However, neither Smith nor Raskob lived to see the building succeed.

At the end of World War II, an army officer piloting a B-25 bomber lost his way to New Jersey. The pilot accidentally flew into the Empire State Building at the 79th floor. Fourteen people were killed. However, the building was relatively undamaged.

The Empire State Building

Symbol of America

Alfred E. Smith had died in 1944. John Jakob Raskob died in 1950. In 1951, the Empire State Building was sold for $34 million. Many people have owned the building since then. They wanted to own the most famous building in New York.

An office in the Empire State Building is a social statement. People all over the world recognize a business's address in the building. The building itself is an image of strength and power.

The Empire State Building is part of the nation's **culture**. The movie *King Kong* was filmed there. A trip to New York City is not complete without a visit to the 86th-floor observation deck.

An inflatable King Kong sat atop the Empire State Building as part of the 50th-anniversary celebration of the movie.

The lightning rod on the tower of the Empire State Building is struck by lightning more than 100 times a year.

The Empire State Building

Standing Tall

In 1972, the Empire State Building lost its title as the world's tallest building. That year, the twin towers of the World Trade Center took the record at more than 1,300 feet (396 m) tall.

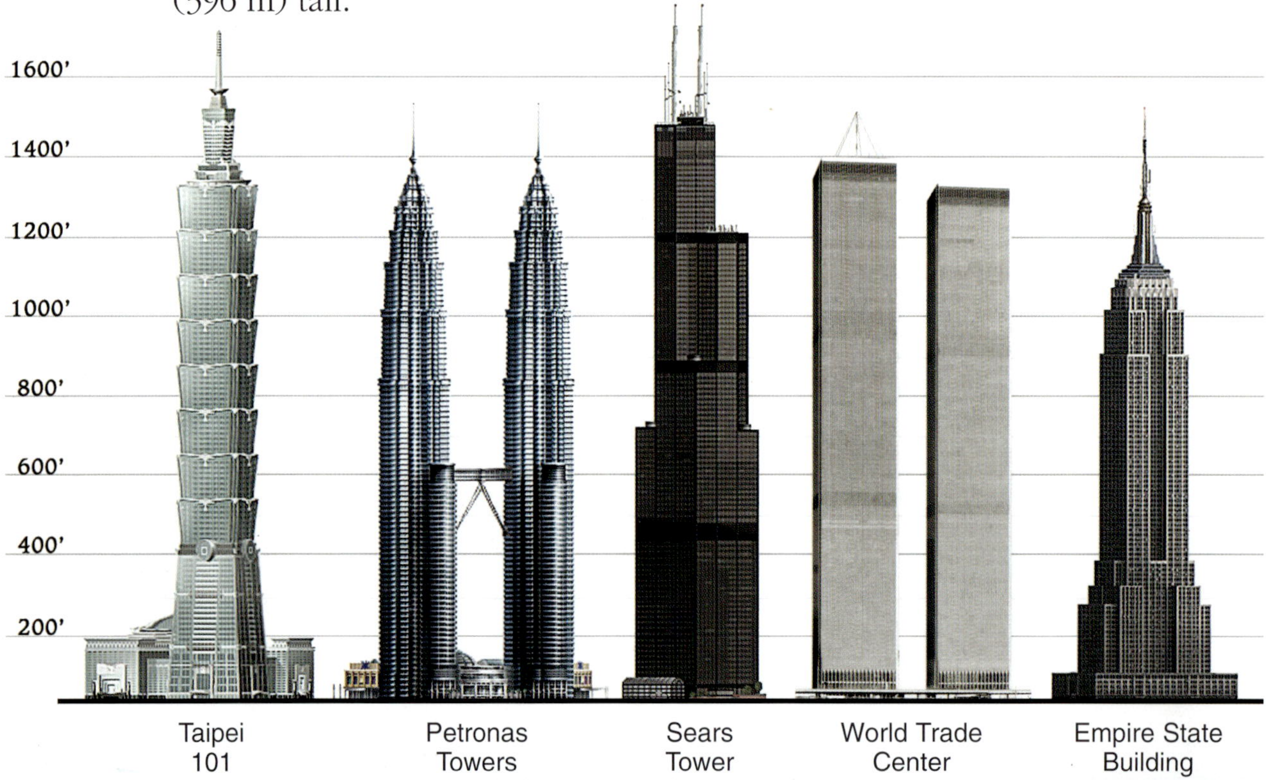

| Taipei 101 | Petronas Towers | Sears Tower | World Trade Center | Empire State Building |

People are still looking to build even taller buildings. Plans are in the works in Hong Kong and India for buildings that will surpass Taipei 101 within the next five years.

Today, there are many buildings taller than the Empire State Building. The tallest building in the world, Taipei 101, is in Taiwan.

But, the Empire State Building will always stand tall and proud. In 1986, it was recognized as a national historic landmark by the National Park Service. It is a landmark, a **cultural** icon, and a symbol of **ingenuity** and achievement in the face of hardship.

American flags fly near the Empire State Building. Many people look to this national landmark as a symbol of American greatness.

Glossary

architect - a person who plans and designs buildings. His or her work is called architecture.

credit - payment for goods and services that are sold on trust.

culture - the customs, arts, and tools of a nation or people at a certain time.

default - failure to pay money that is owed.

demolish - to tear down or destroy.

economy - the way a nation uses its money, goods, and natural resources.

foresight - showing skill and good judgment when making decisions about the future.

girder - a level structural unit that supports an upright load, typically used in the construction of a building or bridge.

Great Depression - a period (from 1929 to 1942) of worldwide economic trouble when there was little buying or selling, and many people could not find work.

ingenuity - skill or cleverness when designing or planning something.

mortgage - money that is owed on a piece of property.

revenue - the total income produced from a given source.

rivet - to fasten with a bolt of metal, typically used to secure two beams into place.

stock - money that represents part of a business. People who purchase stock can own part of the company.

story - the space in a building between two floor levels.

unique - being the only one of its kind.

World War II - from 1939 to 1945, fought in Europe, Asia, and Africa. Great Britain, France, the United States, the Soviet Union, and their allies were on one side. Germany, Italy, Japan, and their allies were on the other side.

Web Sites

To learn more about the Empire State Building, visit ABDO Publishing Company on the World Wide Web at **www.abdopub.com**. Web sites about the Empire State Building are featured on our Book Links page. These links are routinely monitored and updated to provide the most current information available.

Index

A
Astor family 12

B
Bank of Manhattan Building 15
Bethlehem Engineering Corporation 12

C
construction 18, 20, 21

D
Democratic Party 11
design 14, 16
du Pont, Pierre S. 10

E
Empire State Inc. 13, 14, 16, 24

G
General Motors Corporation 10, 11
Great Depression 4, 24

H
Hoover, Herbert 11

I
Indiana 20

K
King Kong 26

L
Lockport, New York 9

M
Metropolitan Life 24
money 12, 13, 21, 24, 25, 26

N
National Park Service 29
New York City, New York 4, 8, 12, 22, 24, 26
New York Life Building 15

O
observation deck 4, 22, 26

P
Pacific Northwest 20
Pennsylvania 20

R
Raskob, John Jakob 9, 10, 11, 12, 14, 22, 24, 25, 26

S
Shreve, Lamb & Harmon 12, 14
Smith, Alfred E. 8, 9, 10, 11, 13, 14, 15, 22, 24, 25, 26
Starrett Brothers & Eken 15, 20

T
Taipei 101 29
tallest building 4, 13, 28, 29
tenants 16, 22, 24, 25, 26

W
Waldorf-Astoria Hotel 12, 14, 18
Waldorf-Astoria Office Building 12, 14
World Trade Center 28
World War II 24, 25

JAN 2 4 2006
$22.78 17(14)